MARGRET & H. A. REY's

Curious George

Visits the Library

Illustrated in the style of H. A. Rey by Martha Weston

WALKER BOOKS

AND SUBSIDIARIES

LONDON · BOSTON · SYDNEY · AUCKLAND

First published in Great Britain 2008 by Walker Books Ltd
87 Vauxhall Walk, London SE11 5HJ

6 8 10 9 7 5

Copyright © 2003 Houghton Mifflin Company
Curious George ® is a registered trademark of Houghton Mifflin Company.
Published by arrangement with Houghton Mifflin Company

This book has been typeset in Gill Sans MT Schoolbook.
Illustrated in the style of H.A.Rey by Martha Weston

Printed in China

British Library Cataloguing in Publication Data:
a catalogue record for this book is available from the British Library

ISBN: 978-1-4063-1407-6

www.walker.co.uk

This is George.

He was a good little monkey and always very curious.

Today George and his friend the man with the yellow hat

were at the library.

3

George had never been to the library before. He had never seen so many books before, either. Everywhere he looked, people were reading.

Some people read quietly to themselves.

But in the children's room the librarian was reading out loud.

It was story hour!

George loved stories. He sat down with a group of children to listen.

The librarian was reading a book about a bunny.

George liked bunnies.

Behind the librarian was a book about a dinosaur. George liked dinosaurs even more. He hoped she would read it next.

But next the librarian read a book about a train.

George tried to sit quietly and wait for the dinosaur book to be read.

But sometimes it is hard for a little monkey to be patient.

When the librarian started a story about jungle animals, George could not wait any longer. He had to see the dinosaur book. He tiptoed closer.

"Look, a monkey!" shouted a girl.

The librarian put her finger to her lips. "We must be quiet so everyone can hear," she said nicely.

"But there's a monkey!" said a boy.

The librarian nodded and smiled. "Mmm-hmm," she agreed.

When she finished reading the jungle story,
the librarian reached for the dinosaur book.
Where did it go?
And where was George?

George was all ready to take the dinosaur book home and read it with his friend when another book caught his eye . . .

10

This book was about trucks.

George wanted to take it home, too!

And here was a book about elephants.

George loved elephants. He added it to his pile.

11

George found so many good books, he soon had more than he
could carry. He leaned against a shelf to rest.

Squeak, went the shelf.

"Shhh!" said a man.

Squeak, went the shelf again — and it moved! Why, it wasn't really a
shelf after all. George had found a special trolley for carrying books.

What luck! Now George could carry all the books he wanted.
He rolled the trolley between the shelves and stacked up books
about boats and kites and baking cakes. He climbed higher to
reach books about cranes and planes.

At last George had all the books he could handle. He couldn't wait to head home and start reading. And right in front of him was a ramp leading to the door. George was curious. Could he roll the trolley all the way home?

Down the ramp George went. The trolley rolled faster and faster. "Stop!" a library volunteer shouted. "Come back here with my trolley!" But George was too excited to listen. The trolley was picking up speed, and George was having fun!

Until – CRASH! – George and the trolley ran
smack into a shelf of encyclopedias.
Books flew up in the air.
And so did George! He landed in a big pile
right between O and P.

"Oh no!" moaned the volunteer when he saw the mess George had made. "How am I going to put away all of these books?"

"I'd like to borrow this one," said a boy from story hour.

"And I'll take this one," said a girl.

With help from George and the children,
the books were sorted in no time. Soon there
was just a small pile of George's favourites left.

"Would you like to take those books home with you?"
the volunteer asked George. Then he took George to a
special desk and helped him get his very own library card.

George was holding his brand-new card when his friend arrived
with a stack of books of his own. "There you are, George!" he said.
"I see you are all ready to check out."
George and his friend gave their books to the librarian.
She smiled when she saw George's pile. "I was wondering where
this dinosaur book went," she said. "It's one of my favourites, too."
The librarian stamped the books and handed them back to George.

With his books under one arm,
George waved goodbye to the
volunteer, the librarian, and
the children from story hour.

22

"Come and see us again, George,"
the librarian said, waving back.
"Enjoy your books!"

And he did.

The end.